Dear Parent:
Your child's love of reading starts here!

Every child learns to read in a different way and at his or her own speed. Some go back and forth between reading levels and read favorite books again and again. Others read through each level in order. You can help your young reader improve and become more confident by encouraging his or her own interests and abilities. From books your child reads with you to the first books he or she reads alone, there are I Can Read Books for every stage of reading:

SHARED READING
Basic language, word repetition, and whimsical illustrations, ideal for sharing with your emergent reader

BEGINNING READING
Short sentences, familiar words, and simple concepts for children eager to read on their own

READING WITH HELP
Engaging stories, longer sentences, and language play for developing readers

READING ALONE
Complex plots, challenging vocabulary, and high-interest topics for the independent reader

ADVANCED READING
Short paragraphs, chapters, and exciting themes for the perfect bridge to chapter books

I Can Read Books have introduced children to the joy of reading since 1957. Featuring award-winning authors and illustrators and a fabulous cast of beloved characters, I Can Read Books set the standard for beginning readers.

A lifetime of discovery begins with the magical words "I Can Read!"

Visit www.icanread.com for information
on enriching your child's reading experience.

To Ethan Zarella and
Max Honig, my Power
Lunch pals
—J.O'C.

For my friends from the
Pennsylvania Ballet
—R.P.G.

For Script-Doctor L.B.:
This amazing Umpteenth
Act is all your doing
—T.E.

HarperCollins®, ☰®, and I Can Read Book® are trademarks of HarperCollins Publishers.

Library of Congress Cataloging-in-Publication Data
O'Connor, Jane.
   The show must go on / by Jane O'Connor ; cover illustration by Robin Preiss Glasser ; interior illustrations by Ted Enik. — 1st ed.
      p.   cm. — (Fancy Nancy) (I can read! Level 1)
   Summary: Nancy, who likes to use fancy words, is dismayed to be partnered with shy classmate Lionel for the school talent show until she comes up with an act perfectly suited for both of them.
   ISBN 978-0-06-170373-7 (trade bdg.) — ISBN 978-0-06-170372-0 (pbk.)
   [1. Talent shows—Fiction. 2. Schools—Fiction. 3. Vocabulary—Fiction.] I. Preiss-Glasser, Robin. II. Enik, Ted, ill.
III. Title.
PZ7.O222Sh 2009
[E]—dc22
                  2008047701
                  CIP
                  AC

14   15   16   17   18   LP/WOR   10 9 8 7 6 5 4 3   ❖   First Edition

I Can Read!

BEGINNING
1
READING

Fancy NANCY

The Show Must Go On

by Jane O'Connor

cover illustration by Robin Preiss Glasser

interior illustrations by Ted Enik

HarperCollins*Publishers*

"Quiet, please," says Ms. Glass.

"I have an announcement."

(That means she has something

important to tell us.)

"The talent show is in a week."

Yay! Bree and I bump fists.

We have our act planned out already.

We will wear fancy circus costumes.

We will sing a song.

It is about daring girls on a trapeze.

Then Ms. Glass says,

"I am assigning partners."

Oh no!

That means we don't get to choose!

I am not assigned to Bree.

I am assigned to Lionel.

He is very shy.

I hardly know him.

Ms. Glass wants us

to brainstorm with our partner.

That means to talk over ideas.

So I ask Lionel,
"Do you like to sing?"
He says no.
He does not like to dance
or tell jokes.

He can wiggle his ears.

He can crack his fingers.

He can balance a spoon on his nose.

"Very cool," I say.

"But I can't do those things.

We need to perform together."

(Perform is a fancy word for act.)

That night I say,

"Bree and Yoko are partners.

They will do a fan dance

and wear kimonos."

(I explain that a kimono

is a fancy Japanese robe.)

13

"Lionel and I

can't think of anything to do."

I sigh a deep sigh.

"And now I won't get to wear

my circus costume."

Mom says, "Ask Lionel over.

Get to know each other.

It will help you plan an act."

On Saturday I ask Lionel over.

But his mom can't drop him off.

So Dad drives me to Lionel's house.

Ooh la la! It is very fancy.

It is almost a mansion.

Lionel's room is huge.

(Huge is much bigger than big.)

There are lots of toy lions.

"Oh! I get it!" I say.

"You like lions

because your name is Lionel."

I pick up a little glass lion.

"This is adorable," I say.

I tell him I like fancy words.

And adorable is fancy for cute.

Lionel shows me a lion mask.

"Wow," I say. "It's great!"

He puts on the mask.

"Grrr," Lionel says, and chases me.

We race all over his house.

"Help! Help!" I yell.

Later we have snacks.

"You're a great lion," I tell Lionel.

Then I get an extremely great idea!

"Let's do a circus act.

You can be the lion.

I can be the lion tamer.

I already have a costume."

Lionel likes the idea. Yay!

The next week we get together

many times to rehearse.

(That's a fancy word for practice.)

Still, we are nervous
on the day of the show.
We hear Ms. Glass announce,
"Here is Lady Lulubell
and the man-eating lion!"

The curtain opens.

Lionel jumps through the hoop.

Lionel walks on a pretend tightrope.

Then he roars and chases me.

"Don't eat me!" I cry.

"Eat this instead!"

I hand Lionel a huge lollipop.

He starts licking it and purring.

Then I curtsy and he bows.

Our act is over.

There is a lot of applause!

(That's a fancy word for clapping.)

I hear my dad shout, "Bravo!"

We all go out for ice cream.

I give Lionel a clay lion I made.

And guess what?

He teaches me

to balance a spoon on my nose!

31

Fancy Nancy's Fancy Words

These are the fancy words in this book:

Adorable—cute

Announcement—something important to tell

Applause—clapping

Assign—to choose something for someone else

Brainstorm—to talk over lots of ideas

Bravo—way to go!

Kimono—fancy Japanese robe

Mansion—a very fancy house

Perform—to act (or dance or sing)

Rehearse—to practice